All These Pronouns Jump Bones

Erotic poetry by
S.A. Harper

Word Oyster Press

Poetry is meant to be read aloud. Shout these poems to a mirror when you're alone. Go outside and whisper them to the trees at midnight. Read them to someone else — anyone else — and see who blushes first.

Contents

<u>One</u>

~

"Sex is kicking death in the ass
while singing."
— Charles Bukowski

Our Exhibit

These are the relics of love —
artifacts artfully amiss in afterglow,
the bedcovers covering nothing,
the pillows slumping in exhaustion,
the silent sheets speaking volumes,
their wrinkles, their spots,
the bottom sheet's right corner
pulled loose, the elastic no match
for your fingers' coital clutch.
That my great-grandparents' bed still stands
is evidence of retrofitted springs and slats.
But its new location, five inches from the wall
and beyond the reach of the morning alarm,
is testament to both vector physics
and your exuberant turn on top.

See this, class? This tousled panoply?
This is how the world was
that afternoon in late September —
the moment our exhibit opened,
the instant our history began.

So hang the velvet rope across the doorway.
Alert the guards, the tour guide dressed in blue.
Warm up the IMAX and flip the latch.
Let our patrons in.

C Poem

C is for cookie
and cupcake and cunt.
C is underwire.
It tips on its side and holds your boob up.
(With two Cs you can have cleavage! Huzzah!)

Cunnilingus is a C word, too —
the long, leisurely lapping at
that clit C, rising from its clamlike folds,
cooing juice and clearly cute.

Then again, I could cleave you with a C,
make you cum with my cock,
clasp clutch claw my clavicle.
I could watch you clench and concede,
clearly confounded.

Eventually, C is for cupcake again —
icing and sprinkles and cream in your jeans.
Buy it at the bakery.
Cram it inside your panties.
Crush it between your thighs.
Then come with a C, looking for me
to clean, to claim, to consume.

waterslide

your pinksy nub, nubbin of pink pearl,
pearly pink and pearly wet,
slippery slick and pinkity wet,
warm and slidy slick —
a pinkly slick slide
my tongue shoots down,
slippity slosh,
slurpity splash,
lip-tipping into a splishity pool
of pinkly, pearly you.

Spring Haiku I

A daffodil. Geese
flying north. Soon you can have
sex without wool socks!

≈

The bulb bursts, shaft springs
erect, bobbing in the sun.
Plants do that too, right?

≈

Look the way he melts!
Hasn't chocolate bunny
seen pussy before?

≈

Equal day and night.
We fuck at the tipping point
between dark and light.

Summer Haiku I

Sunlight in my eyes:
shattered by leaves, your red hair,
both above me, swaying.

~

Outdoor etiquette —
should one slap a mosquito
on an upturned ass?

~

Nature's timing stinks.
Twice this week, I must wake you
to fuck in thunder.

~

Relax. Be patient.
Summer sweat makes nylon rope
harder to untie.

The Honesty of an Iconoclast

I want it.
I want it.
I want it.

I want it hard and fast.
I want it low and loose.
I want the bite and the bruise,
two fingers in every hole,
one penis in every pot,
and no time like now.

Women don't think about sex?
Women just want to relate?
Fuck you, you dick-slingin' fuck.

I want it.
I want it.
I want it.

I want your spit and your tongue.
I want your cock and your cum.
I want your skin sticking to me,
grinding on me, rubbing me raw.
I want razor burn on my thighs
and nipples sucked 'til they bleed.

Don't tell me what I want.
Don't mansplain me what I need.

I want my ass grabbed 'til I gape.
I want my legs splayed obtuse.
I want to be pushed against a window
and displayed to the street below —
my face on fogged glass, my flattened tits,
my open hands pushing back
against that brittle clarity.
I want to embody my exhibition
and wave like the Queen 'til I fall.

I'm choking on the throbbing thick timpani,
the Tantalus timer ticking
necessity of my own natural needs.
I've wanted what I want before Lana del Rey,
before you popped into the room like Oz,
before your little man learned to stand up,
before I wore what I wore
and shaved what I shaved,
before tonight and last night and the night
before when I drank and came alone.

Don't doubt me when I say it's now or never.
This wave is an immutable force.
This wave will curl, crash, wash ashore
with or without you and your speckled eyes.

I want what I want.
Tassel on the table, boy. In or out?

Sweet'N Low and the All-Sheer Toe

There are things at the back of my closet
that have been there for decades —
the rarely-worn shoes, sweaters, suits

that no longer fit either me or the times,
their jacket lapels too narrow or too wide,
the weary pinstripes, unloved vests,

pants with cuffs filled with dust.
(Is that dust figurative or literal?
I think that often it's much the same.)

Packing up clothes for Goodwill,
I've found a memory tucked inside a memory.
From the pocket of a tweed sport coat

(itself bought from Salvation Army)
I've pulled out a wad of beige cloth —
the pantyhose with the run, the ones

you tore from your legs in my car
on the way back from dinner theater, shreds
left scattered: front seat, floorboard, dash.

The show was *Hair* and I didn't see the nude scene
because that's when you stole the condiment rack
from our table, fitting the whole thing —

salt and pepper shakers, packs of sweetener,
the chrome wire rack itself — into your bag.
If you were caught, I thought, "Where Do I Go?"

I don't have a memento of the time you
licked vanilla yogurt off my best friend's dick.
He knew enough to feel sheepish, but not you.

We're reckless with memories. We leave them
like tatters, bits of nylon ripped and flung,
perhaps picked up, saved, forgotten in a pocket.

Less empathetic than most, you may have
never noticed your detritus, their effects,
your willing bad stuck to your unintended good.

Fall Haiku I

Your parents wonder
why your hair is full of leaves.
So are my boxers.

~

Mice in the attic:
I pause, mid-stroke, listening.
You protest. They gnaw.

~

I sip hot cider.
You sigh, rope binding your breasts.
How 'bout them apples?

~

The trick in autumn
is removing more clothes. The
treat is obvious.

Winter Haiku I

We have no fireplace.
No bearskin rug, thick and white.
Red, the slapper stings.

～

Pussy on pillars.
Did you think I bought thigh highs
just to keep you warm?

～

Winter. We play inside.
I jack the furnace full blast...
both nude, you in socks.

～

February pale,
your skin hides on crisp white sheets.
Cum and reappear!

Game Face

"Don't," I said, dead set against a facial,
yet somehow still nakedly kneeling,
awkwardly, ambivalently assenting
to an impending tablespoon of jizz

"coming soon" to my open mouth.
It's not even that I mind so much.
I enjoy the eye contact, the drama.
Most times, I even like your taste.

For a while, I watch you yank,
stroke, squeeze that fleshy snake.
Clearly, you know what you're doing.
Does it help if I tickle your balls?

This is not my favorite view.
I like your veiny profile best —
the curve and colors, the thinly-veiled pulse —
not this head-on, tiny blinking hole.

Eyes locked, I try to gauge your progress.
My knees are getting sore.
There've been too many "Oh, yeahs."
Too long with my mouth an O,

my tongue out, waiting, cross-eyed,
hoping your aim isn't bad,
that you won't miss the mark
and squirt spunk up my nose.

My anticipation meets your resolution:
two strong spurts, three fading… and done.
I love to feel your legs buckle.
Coming while standing is a bitch.

You touch my cheek with one hand,
wipe the last drop on my lip with the other.
I have a mouth filled with cum —
warm, concurrently thin and thick.

It doesn't matter what I do now.
I can swallow, dribble, spit it on the ground.
Either way, you're going to help me to my feet.
You're gonna kiss me. You're gonna taste you.

Bestie, My Bae

A thousand days ago, Becca and I
thought ourselves old fashioned and hip —
we were nouveau cool like vinyl records,
like Pop art mini-dresses, poetry, and berets.

Buzzed on M&Ms and the bossa nova,
we vouchsafed our virginities to Jude Law,
froze them in Ziplocs like precooked meals
meant for thawing the night of senior prom.

(I waited. Not to say I didn't let a cellist's fingers
in my capris, wasn't offered an artist's cock
to roll in my hands like a coil of warm clay.
Becca didn't wait. She fucked and that's OK.)

We and our dates bailed on prom two hours in,
having dipped into our college funds for nips
and two adjoining rooms at the Sheraton Chalet.
We arrived sans luggage, humming like blenders.

The guys went for ice and Cokes, returning
to find us sitting cross-legged on a bed, wearing only
their tuxedo jackets, our mall underwear, and smiles —
a combo surely formal enough for this occasion.

We made the guys strip to their boxers
just to see if they could keep from popping out.
After two drinks, no one minded the gaps —
the peeking nipples, panties, the leaky bulges.

True bohemians, we left the door between rooms
open to the lurid, lowlit murmur of our foreplay —
Becca's guy with her, mine nervously with me —
two sets of sheets rustling like condor wings.

He and I had four square meters of ready skin,
so we left the bathroom door cracked, light enough
to see each other, enough light to touch or taste
all that we could see to taste or touch.

I was giddy at his chest, his hard calves,
the way his erection sprang to meet my hand,
how his balls crept in their bag all on their own.
When I turned over, his stubble tickled down my back.

I rocked to my knees, pressed my cheek to the pillow,
raised my ass so he could see all I've ever hidden —
my slit, my fur, all my funny bits and holes.
It wasn't a porn thing. I wanted no secrets.

I wondered if Becca was kissing when I was,
which of them was first to throw a leg over the other,
who was on top, who tore open the wrapper.
I wondered if it was normal for me to wonder.

Yet I was present in my moment, aware of my pulse,
my breathing, his chest rubbing against my breasts,
his cock not yet inside me, a meat-filled balloon
nestled in, slipping and sliding between my legs.

When both air conditioners shut off, the lack of white noise
felt intentional, both rooms amplified for effect.
Becca's laugh, then moans both hers and his.
When it happened for me, I gasped and knew she heard.

Too soon we were stepping on bobby pins,
stepping around condoms and untied ties,
both making our way to one bathroom
to pee and put on our after-party clothes.

We brushed knots from each other's hair
and redid our makeup to look hot,
not even trying to hide our bruised lips,
our flushed chests, our "been there" smiles.

Even the Uber Guy knew,
his "You guys be safe" clearly referring
to both our future and our immediate past.
If Becca and I didn't smell of sex, we glowed.

Moving forward, she and I don't need your
blood-oath bleeding into each other's open wounds.
We've held hands on fuck-rumpled beds.
We've heard each other laugh and come.

captain nemo dines out

leviathan
teeth and tongue
slip through kelp
black coral reef
follow fish
in swirling brine
open oyster
he nibble pink
the trembling pearl

Two

~

"Dinah Kaufman lost her virginity a
total of three times. Not because it was
so large that it took three times to knock
it out, but because she thought losing
your virginity was supposed to mean
something and it took her three strikes
to feel that she was even remotely in the
meaning ball game."
— Carrie Fisher

Kama Sutra

Of all the ways —
diagrams and instructions,
arrows and handstands,
rotations, permutations,
arches, squats, splits,
great impaling trapeze swing lifts
and gentle tangles of knotted limbs
soaked and sliding in latex-safe lube —
you are the best way
to love…

No number.
No page.

When you bend, so do I.
I accommodate the way you overthink,
forcing a metaphorical foot behind your neck.
You open wide to my jokes.
You sit square on my vulnerability
and grind on my self-doubt until you come.

You are that position found
giggling between the lines,
naked in nose glasses,
tickling a French tickler,
lying in ambush
like a queef.

Craigslist Poem: 100% as Found

Hey, you! No strings.
Want to lick my fresh Brazilian?
Hurry before I chicken out.
I am wet. You must travel.

Slide my panties down, caress my curvy rear.
Have me gaping on all fours.
I don't like my pussy eaten.
Your pic gets mine.

I am looking for a penis.
Would like a nice hard one. Hubby doesn't mind.
Maybe a nice, yummy blowjob.
You? Short hair and not too tall.

If you're thick, you can have my ass.
If you're thick, I'll call you Sir.

No time to meet anyone, but I need to get laid.
I want to fuck tomorrow during lunch.
I don't want a stud or hottie. I want you.
I can sit on your face.

Call me a dirty slut.
Slide a finger inside me while I squirm.
I want to be your property, your sex toy.
I like to scream when I fuck.

Spank me hard.
Pull my hair.
I could use my Rabbit for you.
I want to see you spurt.

My cunt is smooth and shaved.
Your cock is mine tonight.

Summer Haiku II

So this is beach sex!
My shoes are not the worst place
where I find sand.

~

In July, we pay
bills naked, drip watermelon
on immodest napkins.

~

Farmers market stall:
I hold up one cucumber.
Knowing glances ensue.

~

Our summer rental:
distant dunes, two lovers strip.
We drink beer and watch.

Fall Haiku II

So many leaves to rake.
You bend, your ass tight in jeans.
This can wait. Let's fuck.

~

The time changes. One
hour extra, one hour repeats.
Get naked. Fall back.

~

Oh, amaryllis!
Stiff, erect, growing daily.
How can I compete?

~

By mid-December,
I know something else that will
taste like pumpkin spice

Gonna Put a Ring On It

We never discussed size, how perfect
your statistically-average dick is for me
until we visited the horse park
and stood in awe before that stallion's schlong —
thick and long, like a baseball bat.

I mean, I'm no Catherine the Great.
I've no need for that reach, that girth,
that chock-a-block with cock,
that tearing me a new one,
that ramming my cervix 'til I cry.

My lovers before you weren't so different —
one longer, one short and dark like blutwurst.
The longer one was curved like a scimitar
and made my belly move from inside
like a fetus doing backflips.

But yours, it nestles in and makes itself at home,
deep enough for me to feel,
thick enough for me to grab
when I clamp those PC muscles down.
It's more than a mouthful, not enough to gag,

It's long enough to reach from front, back, side.
It fits comfortably in my hand.
It finds my clit with each in-and-out.
And when I climb on top, it's up for
whatever angle or speed. It's a damn solid ride.

Face it, yours is my favorite penis.
I back my ass into it while you sleep.
I think of it on my morning jog.
I write poems about it and sing its praises to friends.
Even Goldilocks would think your cock is just right.

Taking Turns

There comes a time for the selfish blow job.
Not 69, not another bed or carpet tumble
where we simultaneously act and are acted upon.
Sometimes you offer and it's OK for me to take.

I want to be the meal, the thing in the bowl,
a noodle to slurp, a nibbled corndog,
the ice cream "Flavor of the Week,"
two melting scoops in a sugar cone.

I want to accept, not actively give.
I want to be licked, not licking.
I want to shut my eyes, lose myself,
and greedily sink into my own darkness.

I want to surrender my will to your hands.
I want to center my senses on your suction,
the friction of your teeth behind your lips,
the poking and teasing of your tongue.

If you'll forgive me this rapacity —
this piggish wallow in no-iron sheets —
I'll forgive you yours in half an hour.
I anticipate a far more giving mood.

Vanessa unbuttoned, *tant mieux*

powder blue veins
(nest of twigs, net of roots),
holding, feeding the twins
who hide beneath bits of lace —
babes in the woods.

Articulate Tidings

Hand, hip…
touch, grip.

What we have are these
unspoken signals, shorthand language,
familiar signs visible in light or dark.
They are as clear under blankets and sheets
as when we're buck naked,
buzzed on weed and Oreos,
fucking in the recessed lighting
on the floor of your cousin's
quiet midnight den.

It's not the touch.
It's the way you say it.
So when I feel your hand grasp my hip bone,
dig your nails in and pull,
I know tonight you want
friction first and foremost —
no hard slap of my balls on your thighs.
You want the shallow in-and-out,
all cock head and contracting hole,
the fluttering gobbling penetration.
You want the fast and steady rhythm
and save that deep-thrust shit
for after you've come
and I'm on my own.

Of course, it works both ways.
Tonight it could be my hand on your hip.
And tonight you might know
the slap of my palm means
turn over, raise your butt,
brace yourself for a fast forced entry,
me quickly inside you, nuts deep.
And that's when one hand becomes two
and what was touch morphs into
me insisting, pulling you back into
each hard harsh forward push,
my hip bones meeting your ass
in thump after thump after thump.

Hand, hip.
Touch, grip.

We say what we need
without words' imprecision,
their double-meaning deceptions
and clarification-seeking delays.
There is no ambiguity
in the grasp and pull,
no ambivalence
in the slap and push.
In the silence, we are never
not speaking.

Winter Haiku II

So many layers!
By the time my hand finds skin,
you have found our key.

≈

Tied beneath the tree,
spread wide with lights and tinsel?
To hell with Santa's cookies!

≈

You hang there, naked.
Your thesis advisor phones.
"No, she's indisposed."

≈

Wind howls. I drink tea.
It warms me, though not as much
as a cock-filled mouth.

Spring Haiku II

Your thumb up my ass
on the first of May explains
this spring in my step.

~

Wide, you spread your cheeks.
This spring's possibilities?
Any hole I choose.

~

Pine tree, your pollen
clogs her nose. What she can't taste,
at last she swallows.

~

You stroke my cock, spill
my seed in tomato flats
we'll plant tomorrow.

The Supermarket Sleeper Awakens

On my best day, I'm no cougar, no MILF,
no object, no predator. I'm not one thing
because I am no thing. Nothing at all.
I am a mother and I have vanished
somewhere between college
and this display of organic kale.

I haven't really ceased to exist,
but no one looks at me just the same.
Like a payphone, no one sees me
because I'm no longer worth seeing.
I'm these raisins that my kids won't eat,
stocked next to nuts, provenance unknown.

I've become Suburban Barbie, that thing
with a Sienna and a hint of crow's feet,
pushing a firetruck shopping cart up Aisle 3.
Why fantasize about what's beneath my skirt?
You can tell from there I have no holes.
I've been sanded smooth and sexless.

Put a 32-year old woman next to a 3-year old
and she becomes invisible, even in tight jeans.
Call it stealth mode or cloaking. Call it what you will.
But my smile, my breasts, my firm ass don't matter.
I'm this butcher's cuntless customer, "Yes ma'am"
spoken to the space that I once filled.

I worry that I'm three "Date Nights" away
from spreading my legs and thinking
of Channing Tatum, Swiffering naked,
the way my husband dreams of chicken wings
laid out on the smooth belly of JLaw
lounging atop a car way too small for car seats.

Well, fuck that, Shaw's Reward Card.
Suck my clit, Produce Manager. I am done.

I'm gonna flash my tits at the school's silent auction,
get nasty with an orange slice at halftime
of next Saturday morning's U6 soccer game.
And forget me wearing panties to Parents Night.
Ms. King can explain her curriculum on the SMART Board
while Aspen's mom and I explore our learning styles
in the post office play center at the back of the room.
Bodily-kinesthetic? I definitely learn by touch.

I'll rub one out and go to the church bake sale,
my hands smelling of pussy and just a bit of soap.
I'll work the booth without a bra, wearing
silver clamps and a heavy metal chain
beneath my white apron and satin blouse.
I'll sway at the table, nipples burning, chain tugging,
and I'll ask "Wanna fork?" when I hand men
their mons-shaped pieces of sticky-sweet pie.

Maybe my insurrection starts today.
Maybe I'll strike a match and see what burns.
How many Tumblr hearts for a selfie of my ass

in front of the Rice Chex or my tits in Dairy?
Surely someone will reblog me getting nasty
with this éclair or that baguette.

See me now, baker boy?
Am I starting to appear?

I am the unerased.

July 4: What the Jaycees Don't Know

What simple celebration, this sex!
Each kiss a star, our shadows striped,
the pillows smoke from rocket shells
and breath like fireworks, exploded light.
Joined freedom to freedom,
all day, my 12-ball Roman candle
shooting sparks into your summer's night.

Three

～

"Fucky-wucky! It's not the simple
pastime it would seem to be."
— Henry Miller

Sexting at Work

I say your thumbs got mad skillz.
You could Snapchat a muddy boot
and still word-fuck me a panty puddle,
a slow-mo waterfall washing
down my tatty office chair.

Half hour in and what's started is started.
Ain't a towel that can tame this now.
A flood's a'comin', boy. Bring a boat.
Hold your breath, tread water,
drink deeply… dig a moat.

Time to put you on airplane mode.
It's ten minutes 'til my staff meeting
and that conference room don't come
with drip trays and Shamwow cushions.
You. Stop. Now.

Weak-ass move, I blinked
when I should have blocked.
The phone shimmies. I shake.
Another damn text I shouldn't open.
Like a fool, I read and gush a bucket.

Elevated

The hand that grips the cord
    flexes open and wide.
Its fingers extend into cool air,
then collapse inward.
They form a fist.
The nails dig into their own palm:
self-inflicted stigmata,
    blood from a shuddering,
    somewhat sweaty stone.

Your toes strain to support
    the weight of your 27 years.
They tire, sink, rebound...
    begin to let go, think twice,
    hallucinate of heels,
        the insides of mouths and inseams.

Stretched taut, the cords grab hold,
    awaken the sinking sleeper.
The rafter creaks
    and you almost surrender a sound.
How your wrists must sting!
How your arms and shoulders must burn!

I offer you a reprieve
    and you accept, as you must.
Defiance and fire have their place
    and that is miles from here
    as the crow flies.

I lift sweet and naked you,
　　help part your legs,
　　　place your tired feet on wooden blocks,
　　　　three feet apart and inches high.

You wobble there, not strong enough
　　to keep the blocks from wiggling,
　　　　one slip from hanging,
　　　　one misstep from collapse,
beads and streams of juice and sweat
gleaming between your legs
　　　like liquid lenses
　　　　reflecting purple, red, and pink.

So strong, so controlled.
You've regained the upper hand.
Your breathing is your own.
You can do this.
You can do this.
You can…

Pyrrhic victory, sweetness.

I pull up a chair and sit,
　　my face so close to your swollen sex.
Can you see, dear heart?
Can you picture the game?
Can you fly like a bird?

I take out the long black feather
　　and begin to play.

Fall Haiku III

Thanksgiving drags on.
Let's ditch my sibs and you can
stuff me like the bird.

~

My tits in flannel:
nipples content... and yet they
anticipate wool.

~

I'm prepared for fall:
condom cornucopia,
old sweatshirts with holes.

~

At last, back-to-school —
dorm bathroom, the naked boys?
This girl's homecoming.

Winter Haiku III

December: my ass
is always cold. You should spank
me until it burns.

～

Thermostat button?
Higher and higher. Naked,
you will thank me soon.

～

Heavy, the comforter
pins us to the bed. Our heads
peek out. Hands? Busy.

～

Midnight, New Year's eve.
No one knows who that champagne
cork has got into.

Sitting on the Docent's Face

What matters in art and sex
is simplicity, the clean line,
the integrity of mind and form.

Take, for instance, my hands
trapping your tight tense wrists,
pinning them to the mattress,

seeing your fingers curl up,
then clench, then open wide.
This distortion is Mannerism.

Distortion plus color equals Fauvism —
think the bright reds of paddled flesh,
the fluorescent pinks I could expose

or the angles formed by ropes —
a Cubist pastiche of limbs tied
to bedposts, skin criss-crossed

with leather straps, metal buckles.
Now add an audience. Have each person
draw on you with Sharpies. Dada.

Your eyes roll back, images blur
into nothing but contrast and light.
Your cock is a snake in my water lilies.

If there were a clock here, it would melt.
Soup cans would become tubes of Astroglide
on canvases of flat white and held breath.

All styles, all schools — specks of color
that blend to form your eyes, my breasts,
a lasting impression tacked to the wall —

a small white card with serif font —
notes on the artists, our chosen medium,
the time it took for us to paint...

the things we tried to say.

Fat Tuesday

We are the Krewe of "Rub My Duckie" —
the tribe of vibe, chums of hum.
Beads for boobs, boobs for beads,
the parade leaves Lubeland,
winds up past Labiaville, and into
your Mid-City snowball stand,
ready and armed for bare.
There are no drums like this,
the banging of our bed
against the neighbor's wall.
There are no second-line
observers, no joiners-in
who hear, but do not see.
There are no throws, no floats,
no celebrities, no masked king,
no clean up trucks all in a row.
Just our sounds. Just this music.
Just the fire of our coital flambeaux.

I admit I'm high, but it's true —
I'm fucking a saxophone.
You are a dream in gold sequins,
my sax in the city.
I'd be more humiliated, except
I'm dressed as a spirochete.
It's Mardi Gras.
These things happen.

The Unquestioning Acceptance of Gravity

On the second night, we traded favors
like bubblegum cards, placed side-by-side.

On the whole, I was a happy camper,
tracing roads not found on any map,
following paths known only to the touch,
the almost instinctual migration south
to your swamp and your flamingos.
It was there I went, carefully
parting cattails and loosestrife,
wise to avoid the blistering bladderwort,
deep and deeper still until I found
the lure of your twilight pitcher plant
into which I abandoned and submerged
my nose, my mouth, my tongue.

Later, when you asked, "Is this good?"
your voice rose up like crickets, like frogs,
like sounds from the bottom of a mossy well —
distant, wet, green and resounding.
From that angle, you were all
hair and half-moons,
round and openly lapping.
I reached to hold your one free hand,
pink and damp, strong and warm,
as if to lift you up —
but it was I who fell.

Nooner

We have an hour, maybe less —
an hour to dive inside
    each other's skin,
an hour to laugh and moan,
an hour to throw off blankets
    and imagined discretion,
an hour that's both
    short and expansive,
    restrictive yet liberating,
    discrete not discreet,
an hour that now has only 58 minutes.

With only 58 minutes,
one doesn't stand on formality.
The clothes must come off
and standing must come to an end.
I hop like a buffoon,
    wrestling a recalcitrant sock.
There are no awards
for sticking the landing.

Your hand is cold.
You hold my cock
    like a drawer pull.
I grip the back of your neck
    like a cello.
Striped muscle cells contract
and the distance between us closes.

Still more than 55 minutes, still
enough time to back you against the wall
where warmth is palpable, skin inevitable.
Our lips have started to touch
in that easy face dance of
    hungry dip and dart,
      move countermove.

Perhaps the clock is internal.
We seem to know how long we have
to kiss, how many minutes remain
after I let you grind your wet desire
against my edgewise wrist,
riding the nub of bone
until my fingers drip.

And yes, there is a bed.
It is a fourth-dimensional wormhole.
There is no other way to explain
how we have enough time
to fuck so many ways.

No time to shower.
You pee. I pee.
We share a soapy washcloth,
and blot ourselves dry.
And with two minutes left,
there's nothing left to do

except to abandon the sock
and start to kiss again.

Spring Haiku III

Our picnic for three —
not even the ants can spoil
my breathless spitroast.

≈

Our private seder:
I hide the afikomen
with the flavored lube.

≈

The head of your cock
peeks purple from white blankets:
crocus in the snow.

≈

The birds chirp loud through
May's open windows. Awake,
we may as well boink.

Summer Haiku III

We pick strawberries,
then drive home, red juice leaking
from your cutoff's crotch.

~

Camping by the lake:
we swim naked in moonlight...
forgot the condoms.

~

Ideal summer sight:
two naked girls sword fighting
with freezer-pop cocks.

~

Julie's top fell off:
volleyball stuff of legends...
but I wasn't there.

MILF Lullaby (with apologies to Tom Lehrer)

Summer holds its breath.
Your kids are away at camp
and your husband leaving for Nawlins,
off to live high on the muffaletta,
attend seminars by steamy day
and just maybe dip his dangle
into cool bayou temptation by night.
No harm, no foul.
That's just the way the Hurricane blows.
We're in Sondheim territory
and the mirror reflects you, reflecting.

Summer also smiles knowingly.
While we're on temptation,
summer knows you've been dipping as well.
Coast soon to clear, your online Don Juan
can finally come to your real-life town.

Briefly, you hesitate at the opportunity.
"Don't answer his email.
Don't accept his chat.
All innocent advances are anything but.
They inevitably lead to parking lot quickies
and weekends long with
        hubris and hummers.
        paddles and pasta salad."
You flick the Looney Tunes conscience angel
from your nightshirt shoulder

like a caterpillar that fell from a tree.
Silly angel, but this is exactly what you want.
You honestly, passionately want to
scrape bottom, plumb depths of delight
in borrowed fuck-me pumps.
You ache to kiss with hunger,
pretend you're starved.
be an upper middle class passion's plaything—
your breasts by Brio,
your Bionicle butt held firm and high.

And so you say yes.
And so you go to the airport.
And so you wait in Baggage Claim —
    emotionally open, physically scared,
suddenly aware that crotchless panties
don't soak up a bit of this trickle,
    this drip,
    this river,
    this flood down your thigh
that surely everyone sees.
But is it really any wonder you're excited?
You've given yourself permission to be
a stranger with this stranger.
It won't be the "you from work"
    wearing that mail-order lingerie,
    the panties split up the back
    to show your pink princess plug.
It won't be the "you from home,"
    tied to the bed with curtain cords,
    spread wide and on display.

And it won't be the "PTO you"
whose hair gets pulled,
    ass spanked,
    nipples twisted red,
    pussy sucked and nibbled
until you cry out his name
that may not even be his name.

Summer leads us astray
and this you that isn't you
has a smile on her face, a light
that you can see in the mirror
as your husband's morning taxi
slowly pulls away from the curb.

train of thought enters a tunnel

park bench sitter draped
in golden hair inches away
reads her forbes and hums

off key eyes of spring
and fall caged behind lashes
tremble lips and blush cheeks

bangle beads and gaping blouse
breasts like bags of change
imagine her holding it

in her mouth lights face
senses lulled by stimuli
die in their sleep as

the park becomes a cigarette
waiting to be lit

Four

~

"She wanted him everywhere, in all
holes at once — she wanted to show him
the real her and not a movie of her."
            — Nicholson Baker

Asking the Bugaboo to Tea

Admit that you are a willing character
in my self-prescribed debauchery,
my didactic preaching to
a spread-eagled, converted choir of one.
You are usually an open mind with open legs.

And yet, even I have noticed that
I've written my cock in your ass
a hundred times more than
the actual shuddering asterisk winks,
the drunken giggling reality gasps
I can count on one slippery hand.

You are audience.
You are victim.
You are cowriter and managing editor.

Face it, lover.
This time, you bought the lube.

Winter Haiku IV

Tipped into a drift,
you laugh, try — but can't get up:
why snow pants have snaps.

~

In winter, cold toes
in warm holes is considered
temperature play.

~

Winter oral sex
means thighs on ears, blankets perched
on my lapping head.

~

Crumbs on my chest, you slide
your sex on mine, chewing bread
still warm — like butter.

Spring Haiku IV

Open window: peepers
mock the sounds you make. Your ass
blooms pink. My hand stings.

~

In the steady rain,
you kneel beneath my slicker.
Now lick my puddle.

~

String tied to my balls:
if the kite won't tug, you will...
in like a lion.

~

Spring sun? Please make my
pussy photosynthesize.
Sunbeam falls. I spread.

Knowing What You Like

They were always "titties"
to my buddy, Bob.
Never boobs or breasts.
Not even tits.
Just titties.

"She had these big ol' titties," he would say,
his eyes wide, his hands cupping imagined heft
as he told me about some woman in his store.
Bob is how I knew about Moira from school.
She couldn't get enough of Bob scuffing her
"little bitty titties" with his whiskers
until their pale skin turned an angry pink,
like the tips of dogwood petals in spring.

Before our town allowed lap dances,
the strippers at the Red Lion Lounge —
I forget their names, but not the G-strings,

the purple lights, the bald bouncer in black —
they would sit with customers between sets,
nursing drinks, working on their quotas.
They saw me, but saw Bob more. Both nice guys,
but Bob loved titties, making him an honest man.

And Bob loved each and every dancer titty —
big, small, droopy or pert, all with their
nipples sized dime to silver dollar.
One drink or four, he always told them so.

He hollered support when they danced
and toasted them when they sat down,
smiled, touched his arm, called him Sugar.
Why should they care what word he used?

The strippers always knew on instinct
that it's better to have a whooping Bob
praise, tip, or suck your titties
than some quiet, dickless Robert
who thinks you're a cunt.

Private Message/AOL Memoriam

The four-way grope-fest in the forum
begins to wear thin as cyber-spit.
I find a yawning smiley in the pulldown
but hold my fire, hold its tongue.

Let me pull you aside
and seek our online alcove.
Let me bracket your breasts
between laughs and winks,
parenthetically pleasure
and nibble each red herring
with biting wit and seductive simile.
Let me whisper my asides
in the long-form colors of secrets,
in the voices of late night abandon.
Let me make you
lose track of time.

Once Net, never met...
we hardly ponder our non-proximity —
the random rendezvous,
the online fuck-and-run.

Fingers skilled in touch typing
find it easy to peel back distance,
erase time, erase imagined introductions
and awkward first encounters.

Words are not awkward.
Words are under our control.
Words create skin from screen,
    lips from luminous phosphors,
    your cunt from my keystrokes,
    my cock from your extended metaphor.

Even the Auto Correct feature
acts as accomplice,
    blotting out moles, scars,
leaving the perfect image
of our moist imagination —
    the perfect taste,
    the perfect sound,
    the perfect joining of me and you,
        again and again.

Do your real legs spread so wide,
your arms hold so strong and close,
your breath come so hard and fast?

You are no less exciting
for being less than real.
You are no less real
for being less known.

Once Net, never met...
both of us as real as my erection,
the pants you've shed at your feet,
my itch to write, your rush to read,
the endless, ceaseless, tireless joy

79

of these words
and this time...
of this me
in this you...

as real as touch,
as real as wet...

as real as
SEND.

The Night the Bed Collapsed

This old brass bed —
    with its cannon-ball posts,
    its scratches, its broom-handle dents —
has been in this room for 82 years.

This bed has history.
It's seen things.
It's been moved and covered
    when the walls got painted,
    once yellow, three times white.
It's had mattress after mattress.
This bed has seen sex and sickness,
    childbirth and death.
This bed has withstood the circus act
    and the ceiling-touch bounces
    of my sister's twins.
This is a solid bed.

So who would have thought that
the addition of one Jennifer —
130 pounds sans clothes —
would bring down the house?

Who knew our first threesome
could get more awkward?

Viaduct (No Chicken)

When I was younger, I was embarrassed
by the outward manifestations
of my adolescent arousal —
the alarm clock fecundity so obvious
in the way I throbbed like a teen,
the way I swelled and dripped my age.

A boy would brush his arm against me
and I could see my excited snail-self
leaving a trail of slime down C Hall.
I walked, covering my junk with a book,
a hoodie, my hands. I just knew
the janitor was mopping in my wake.

I would ooze into Algebra II and sit
amongst twenty other snails —
a potential orgy of excess genitals and
cross-fired, calcified love darts.
Snails are unrepentant hermaphrodites.
We would have fucked anything that moved.

Turns out, youth is horny, but myopic.
In a teen's thick thicket, she sees
only her spindly, new-growth trees
and her seasonal, intermittent stream,
never her true forest, her sparkling river,
the way her body gleams like an iPhone.

A few years older, I own my river now.
I won't obfuscate. I can't cover and hide.
If you slip your hand inside my pants
and find what's there a sopping sluice,
you'll know the invitation's real:
there's no compliment like lubrication,

no more certain sign than damp Underoos —
my vulva's sweat, my pussy's spigot,
your erection tip's leaky pen, drawing
a small dark spot on the bulge in your jeans.
These are all rain falling on the same side
of a divide, rushing down to the same sea.

Imagine my desire, so succulent
that I need a towel between my thighs.
Then imagine me waving that towel,
heavy and dark, in a crowd, in a fire,
in your face where you can smell the water.
Imagine how you'll cross to the other side.

Summer Haiku IV

Floor and window fans
disguise my vibrator's sound...
but not what comes last.

~

Then there was the time
in P-town, you wore a leash.
Not the strangest thing.

~

Go on, read to me.
Get me drenched? All-access pass
to my waterpark.

~

Hot, no clothes for days.
Your princess plug sparkles blue —
icy butt bauble.

Fall Haiku IV

Grown-up Halloween:
threesome with fun-size redhead...
jack-o-lantern grins.

~

Red orange yellow:
leaves rustle, you give me head
behind bales of hay.

~

Fall's here. Blanket time.
And without the furnace cranked?
No face-sitting soon.

~

Outside, our first frost:
inside, over my knee... slap
pink your harvest moon.

Thirty-one Flavors over Wellfleet

The taste of your taste
is a sideways glance to port,
a heave and a yaw,
slipping down into ocean's nuance,

a bit of salt and sugar
and lemon and sweat.
It's a taste that sneaks about
the fresh-shucked slick of an oyster.

(Or maybe — on land — it's found beneath
the skin of a peeled concord grape —
that green under the purple,
the fun house eyeball never tongued.)

Licking up, north of the mark, your center
presents itself as pebble, as uncooked pea,
a tricky trinket gently tossed between
folds of warm fruit roll-up foam.

It bobs like a buoy, riding ripples
made by breath crossing water,
made by sounds rasped in air,
made wholly of exaltations erupting

from sheets wet with communion,
keening from the grey-green sea to the blue sky
and the heavens where God hears its name
spoken with love and passing tumescence.

We wash ashore in the kitchen, content
to bask in a secular snack of ice cream,
cold pink kisses, and the laughing threat
of chilled spoons on flushed bare skin.

It's Worse with Two Sugars

I told you my iced coffee is strong.
Even cut in half with milk,
slowly diluted by melting ice,
it's a right jarring jolt to the system:
    a cymbal played in a sleeping ear,
    a shower suddenly cold when someone flushes,
    a jalapeno hidden in a melty pool of Jack.

Of course, you've downed half a Grande
before you realize I am again an honest man
and your insides feel like a silver-bullet vibe
rattling around the inside of a julep cup.
I told you to take it slow.
I told you it would last for hours.
I told you to follow me to the back of the park
where the trees are dense and the birds look butch.

You carry your sandals and walk barefoot.
Where I point, you wander.
Behind a sycamore, we stop and hide.
"I have work in half an hour," you tell me
in a buzzy rush of words, twirling on your toes,
ice still rattling in the plastic cup
with its phallic straw and see-through lid.

On the clock, you take my four hard kisses.
You straddle my knee that lifts you up
and backs you against the tree.
You drop the shoes and you drop the cup.

You turn around. You brace.
You find my fingers on your face
instead of bark. So you suck.

The birds see your dress hiked up,
your briefs half-cheek down.
From behind, my middle finger and thumb
slip slickly between your legs
and quickly jam in each caffeinated hole.
You see, this is my tuning fork in reverse.
With these two tines, I can feel
your insides hum.

About the Writer

S.A. Harper hails from somewhere south of the Mason-Dixon line and somewhere unfortunately too far north for a decent oyster po' boy. Harper's first erotic story was written in middle school and involved a distracted and inattentive graduate student, several maraschino cherries missing from their jar, and a telltale trail of sticky pink running down a lover's pale white thigh.

There is a slight possibility that Harper isn't so much an erotic writer as a writer in need of a hearty snack.

For other work by S.A. Harper,
please visit:

Word Oyster Press
wordoyster.com

You may contact the writer at:
saharper@wordoyster.com

www.ingramcontent.com/pod-product-compliance
Lightning Source LLC
Chambersburg PA
CBHW020330130626
46549CB00003B/1101